TERRY DEARY

Saxon Tales

The Shepherd Who Ate His Sheep

Illustrated by
Tambe

BLOOMSBURY EDUCATION
AN IMPRINT OF BLOOMSBURY

LONDON OXFORD NEW YORK NEW DELHI SYDNEY

Contents

1

Hunger

I whine. I grumble and complain. I moan, I grouse, I gripe.

Well, that's what my wife Gladys always used to say. She said it one winter day. I remember the day well. It was the day before our Edward was arrested and sent to be hanged. 'Upton Medway,' Gladys said that day, 'you are a whiner, a grumbler, a complainer.'

'How dare you say that? I have never whined in my life.'

'You're doing it now,' Gladys said.

'No I am not. It is so unfair to call me a complainer,' I complained.

'You are also lazy, idle and a shiftless, workshy waster,' she went on.

'Ah. No, ah, see, you're wrong there, wife. Aha. I can't be shipless...'

'Shiftless.'

'I can't be that either. I don't even know what it means so I can't be that,' I said and I smiled through the smoke from the fire that rose up in our house and tried to escape through a hole at the top.

She stirred the pot of vegetable soup. They were just scraps she'd picked up from the market the day before. 'What is for dinner, my sweet angel?' I asked her.

'Pea and ham soup,' she said.

I smacked my lips. 'Lovely. Where did you get the ham?'

'I didn't,' she snapped. 'It's pea and ham soup... without the ham. I couldn't buy any ham. Why not? I'll tell you why not. Because I didn't have any money. Why didn't I have any money? Because you are too shiftless to go out and earn any.'

I sighed, 'It's not my fault, my little pot of honey. I'm a shepherd. I can't go out shepherding in the snow. I'd catch a cold.'

Gladys pulled the iron ladle out of the green gloop in the pot. She waved it at me, 'No? Then why have you sent our son Edward out into the hills?'

'He's young,' I explained. 'Lads like Edward don't feel the cold the way an old man like me does. I only have to sit down for five minutes in the snow and my bones ache enough to make me cry with pain.'

Gladys waved the ladle and dripped pea

soup over the earth floor. Such a waste.
'First,' she said, 'you are whining again.
And secondly, it isn't snowing.'

'Ah, yes. No. Not yet. But it's cold. And
Odell the wise man says there's snow on
the way.'

The hot ladle dripped a finger-width
from my nose. 'Until you go out and make
some money it's pea soup every day,' she
said. That wasn't quite true. There was
some round, flat bread roasting on the

hearthstones. My mouth was starting to dribble as I smelled it.

The door creaked and a cold wind struck the back of my neck. I shivered. After all I was thirty years old and my blood was too thin to warm me through the winter now. I'm not a complainer, but that lad Edward had to learn to come in the house without letting a winter wind whip the logs and send hot ashes swirling in the air.

'Shut that door, you useless lump,' I groaned. 'You'll set fire to the roof if those sparks fly up.'

'Sorry, Dad,' Edward said. His lips were purple with the cold and his nose red-tipped and dribbling. He wore a coat made from the fleece of a sheep. I got that for him. Or rather I found the dead sheep in a ditch and skinned it before the owner found it was missing. Gladys sewed it into

11

a coat for the lad. The meat and bones gave us mutton stews for a month.

The thought of mutton stew made the pea soup seem feeble fare. I got it into my head that I had to have more mutton. You know how it is. You try to think of something else – anything else. But your gut keeps telling you, over and over, 'Mutton stew. Get me some mutton stew.' And when your gut orders you have to obey.

Hunger. That's what started Edward on the road to the gallows.

2
Cold

Gladys gathered fallen branches and we had a warm fire the next night. 'Poor Edward,' she said as she rubbed her hands together in front of the glowing crimson embers.

'Poor Edward? You sent him off with bread and cheese. He eats better than I do, that lad.'

'He works harder and earns more than you do,' Gladys reminded me. 'Thane Hugh says he's the best shepherd in the village.'

I had to smile. 'No, Gladys my cherub, I am the best shepherd in the village. Edward is second-best. Anyway he is well fed and he has that snug little shepherd's hut on the hillside.'

'Snug?' Gladys gasped. 'It's icy in this weather. And he doesn't spend much time inside. He has to keep going out – whatever the weather – to check there are no thieves

about. They'll cut a lamb's throat quick as the shake of a rat's tail.'

'Ah,' I nodded and thought of that lamb, trimmed and boiling in the pot. 'You're right, Gladys. The lad needs a fire in that hut of his. I'll take him some of the wood you gathered this afternoon.'

'Upton Medway, do you have a fever?'

'No.'

'Have the wood sprites stolen away your wits then?'

'No.'

'Have you been drinking mead from the thane's cellars?'

'No.'

'Then why are you going out on a January night to take our son some wood?' she demanded.

I sighed. 'It's like you say, he's a good lad and the second-best shepherd in the county of Kent. We should look after him.'

'But you never go out after dark in winter. You are up to something, Upton Medway.'

'Yes. I am up to doing good. I am up to helping a cold child on a lonely hill, frightened of losing a sheep to thieves or wolves. Our dear child, helpless and chilled. He needs an angel of mercy to rescue him. And, Gladys, I am that angel.'

My wife's jaw was dropping slack and her eyes were filling with tears. 'Oh, Upton... that's the man I married. A caring soul with the heart of a hero. Go forth and rescue our child. I'll pray you aren't attacked along the dark roads by wild beasts or wilder men.'

When she put it like that I wasn't so keen. Then I thought of the poor little lambs. I took a carving knife from the table... in case I was set upon by guard dogs or madmen, owls or churchyard ghosts. I wrapped a woollen cloak around my shoulders, gathered some firewood and stepped into the icy night wind.

The village was quiet. A watchman wandered the road between the houses, crying 'Eleven o'clock and all's well'.

He swung his lantern from side to side. I hid behind a garden wall. I was on a mission of mercy. Old Drew wouldn't have arrested me for being out after curfew. Not if I told him I was an angel of mercy. But I didn't want an old friend to get into trouble for letting me pass.

When the road was clear I splashed along the slushy road and felt the wetness seep into my boots.

From the top of the hill I could see a glow of torches from the town of Maidstone on the coast. They didn't go to bed so early in the towns. But a wicked wind whipped over the waves and turned my fingers numb.

Still, the journey was worth it. I returned to the house with a fresh leg of mutton. Some ruthless thief had cut the throat of a sheep and hacked off the leg.

Oh, but the broth dear Gladys made for us the next day was better than the food of the gods.

It was going to taste bitter before nightfall when we discovered the trouble it brought poor Edward.

3
Prison

The curfew bell had rung. Edward had set off to guard the sheep by night. His belly was full but he was unhappy as a fox in a field full of hounds. 'There was a sheep missing this morning, I'm sure of it,' he said for the tenth time that day. 'Where did you get that leg of mutton, Dad?' he asked.

'I found it in a ditch when I brought you that firewood last night,' I told him for the tenth time.

'Lord Hugh will surely sack me if it's from his flock,' he sighed.

'It could be from any of the thanes in Kent. A stray. You have nothing to worry about. Nothing at all.'

Sometimes you say something and it brings down a curse upon your head. As soon as I said, 'You have nothing to worry about,' there was a thunderous knock on the door that almost shook it off its leather hinges. 'Open up, Medway,' came the voice of Thane Hugh.

I lifted the latch and he burst in with two men-at-arms who filled the room with weapons and menace. I was shivering. I am not a coward, you understand. Just cold.

'Shut the door, Thane Hugh,' Gladys snapped.

One of his men kicked it shut with his iron-studded boots. 'Edward Medway,' he said to my son. 'I am arresting you on a charge of stealing a sheep. You will be tried by the magistrate tomorrow

morning. He will find you guilty and you will hang.'

Thane Hugh was as fat as one of his pigs and smelled no better. Gladys turned pale even in the amber glow of the fire.

'How do you know the magistrate will find him guilty?' she asked.

'Because I have decided he is guilty. I pay him well to care for my sheep. We found one this afternoon, half hidden in bushes. If it hadn't been for the crows pecking at the body it might have stayed there till summer.'

Now I enjoyed going to the court and hearing the villains of Kent going on trial. I am a clever man – my mother always told me. And I learned one or two tricks that the lawyers used. I was ready for this one.

'Aha, Thane Hugh. If my Edward stole a sheep, why did he hide it in the bushes, eh? It doesn't make sense.'

He turned his ugly, bear-eyed face

to me. 'Because he's too skinny to drag it back to the village, you ignorant little man.'

I wasn't going to be bullied. 'In that case why would he kill it if he couldn't bring it home. Eh? Answer me that?'

The thane looked at me tiredly. 'The sheep we found had a back leg missing. The lad hacked it off and carried it home this morning.'

'Aha, prove it,' I said.

Thane Hugh walked over to our cooking put and sniffed it. 'Mutton broth.' The stew was cold now since we'd eaten and taken the pot off the fire. The thane put a hand in and pulled out some bones... the bones

from the leg of a sheep. 'Proof enough?' he asked nastily. He turned to his men. 'Take the boy away and shut him in the animal pound for the night.' (He meant the stone hut where stray animals were kept till their owners claimed them. The villagers used it as a prison.)

The men grabbed an arm each and dragged the whimpering boy out. 'Don't worry, son,' I called after him. 'I'll be in court to defend you tomorrow.'

Thane Hugh turned to me and smirked. 'That's good. You can come along to the hanging afterwards. Goodnight. Sleep well,' he said and marched out after his men.

'Shut the door,' Gladys shouted.

He didn't.

4

Court

'Edward Medway,' the magistrate said, 'you are charged with the crime of stealing one of Thane Hugh's sheep. Are you guilty or not guilty?'

My son's bottom lip trembled and his tongue seemed suddenly too large for his mouth.

I rose to my feet. 'He is not guilty, your worship,' I said with a humble bow to the great man from the bishop's palace.

'Who are you?'

'Upton Medway, your holiness. Edward's father.'

The man's pinched face was sour. 'You wish to speak for the guilty boy?'

'He's not guilty yet,' I said.

'Don't try to be clever and put me right,' the magistrate said and his voice was a low rumble like thunder. 'The mutton was eaten by you so there may be a case for letting you hang alongside your son. Would you like that, Upton Medway?'

'No, your holiness,' I said and my voice seemed to rise as high as a boy in the monks' choir.

'Then state your case.'

I had lain awake the past night talking this through with Gladys. We had our defence ready. I looked through the crowds of villagers who had gathered in the thane's great hall and saw my wife. She gave a small smile and a nod. I cleared my throat.

'Edward Medway is an honest lad. He is also the second-best shepherd in the village. When he was a child he found a silver coin in the roadway. Any other lad would have slipped it into his sleeve and spent it. But what did honest little Edward do?' I asked.

The crowd nodded, and murmured. But the magistrate picked up his walking cane and smashed it on the table in front of him. What has this to do with stealing a sheep?'

I was flustered, I must admit. 'Nothing, but...'

'Then get on with your defence. Edward Upton killed one of his own sheep. He cut off its leg and carried the leg home. Thane Hugh found the bones for himself. How do you explain that?'

'I'm glad you asked me that, your worshipfulness,' I said with another small bow.

'And I'll be glad if you give me an answer,' the magistrate said. 'If the wicked lad didn't kill the sheep then who did?'

'A wolf, Your Grace,' I said.

That caused a sensation in the court. Voices cried in fear and churls like myself who kept animals were in a panic.

The magistrate rolled his eyes so he was looking up at the thatch on the roof of the hall. 'Has anyone seen a wolf in Kent in the last fifty years?' he asked.

The villagers just looked at their boots and shook their heads.

'And have you seen this wolf, Upton Medway?' the bishop's man asked.

'Not exactly,' I said.

'Not *exactly*? What does that mean? You either did or you didn't.'

'I thought I saw something moving in the shadows... like a big dog.'

He gave me that sharp look again. 'So you were there?'

'Yes,' I said.

The magistrate exploded with rage and waved his cane at me the way Gladys waved her ladle. 'It was a dark and moonless night. If there is no light there is no shadow,' he roared. 'You forget I have seen this dead sheep. The leg was cut off cleanly with a knife. The throat was cut with a knife.' Suddenly he leaned forward and looked at me with eyes like nails.

'Tell me Upton Medway, how many wolves have you met that carry knives.'

A soft chorus of giggles ran round the hall. The case was not going well. I cleared my throat again. 'Well... maybe it was thieves. Not my son... sheep thieves. They killed it and cut off its leg.'

The magistrate did that rolling eye thing again. 'Medway,' he said slowly speaking as you would to a child of three. 'The leg was found in your house. How do you explain that?'

'Maybe the thieves dropped it,' I muttered.

'What? These thieves are so useless they kill a sheep, carve off its leg, then get so careless they leave the body in the bushes and drop the tastiest piece – the leg – in the field. Why would they do that?'

I shrugged. 'Maybe they were disturbed when I took my son some firewood. That's how I came across the leg of mutton.'

The magistrate smiled. 'So you took the mutton home and that's how it got in your pot.'

'Yes sir.'

'Your son killed the sheep and you helped him.'

'Yes, sir... I mean no, sir.'

'Invisible wolves or stupid thieves. I believe none of this nonsense. I find Edward

Medway guilty as charged. I sentence him to hang on the village green at sunrise tomorrow morning.'

Gladys was glaring at me. I gave her a weak smile. I guess that didn't go too well.

5
Gallows

The villagers were excited. They didn't often get to see an execution in their own market square. They were planning to have a special fair with games to entertain the children and gambling for the fathers and sports for the youths. It would be a public holiday.

As they crowded, chattering, to the door of the hall one voice cried out over the others. 'I appeal.'

The hall fell silent. The magistrate looked up, 'Who said that?'

Old Drew stepped into the middle of the hall. 'I'm the watchman, Drew Smith, sir. I've been working in the law business for thirty years. And I know a convicted man or woman or child has a right to appeal to Bishop Theodred.'

'Appeal? You mean get the bishop to overturn my decision?'

'Yes, sir.'

'Are you saying I am wrong?' the magistrate raged.

'No sir,' Drew said and stood firm. 'I am saying the bishop may speak to God and God may have a different way of doing things.'

The magistrate chewed on his fingernail and thought about arguing with God. 'You have a day to get to the bishop's palace and a day to return with his decision. If you are not here in two days the boy will hang.' The man stormed out of the hall, pushing the churls aside.

As Edward was led back to the compound I hurried across to Drew. 'Thank you, my friend. I will come with you.' I looked across at Gladys who was wiping her nose on her sleeve. 'Make us some bread and cheese and mead for the journey.'

She sniffed away the last of her tears. 'Don't let our Edward down again,' she said.

'What do you mean *again*?'

She looked at me through red-rimmed,

angry eyes. 'You know what I mean. Now hurry. It's a day's walk to the bishop's palace and another day back. Hurry.'

I hurried. Old Drew was a slow walker, the roads were heavy with mud as the snows melted a little. We plodded on mostly in silence. It was dark by the time we reached Maidstone and our first problem.

A row of royal guards blocked the road to the palace. 'No one enters,' an officer with a face of stone said.

'We must see the bishop. It's a matter of life and death.'

'Pah,' the guard snorted. 'They all are. But the king arrives tomorrow morning and no one enters the palace till he's gone.'

'But we *have* to see him. If we don't see him my son dies,' I moaned.

The man shrugged his huge shoulders and his armour rattled. He prodded my shoulder with a fat finger. 'Then your son dies. Now clear off or you'll be joining him... on the end of my sword.'

We turned and trudged away. An ox-cart splashed past, loaded with vegetables for the palace kitchens. It had a loose cover of waxed cloth over it to keep the stuff dry. Drew and I looked at one another. Without a word we lifted the cover, and climbed among the fresh cabbages and carrots, parsnips, and leeks, turnips and onions.

There was fruit there too. Apples and pears. The bishops and the kings of the world lived well. They wouldn't miss a couple of apples, I decided, as I chewed on one and the cart clattered past the guard.

We slipped out as the cart halted outside the kitchen doors and stood at the back. Drew may have had an old head but it was a wise one. Instead of running and hiding, he stood there. As the carter stepped off the cart Drew grinned and called, 'Greetings, friend. We've been waiting for you.'

The farmer was as shrivelled as one of his apples left in the sun too long, and just as sour. 'I hope the cook sent you here to help me unload this lot?'

'He did,' I said and began to unload the baskets of fruit and vegetables.

Inside the kitchen scullions were filling copper pots and boiling beefs, legs of mutton and pork. They were stuffing sausages and making milk puddings with honey.

A huge man with a belly like a walrus was shouting orders. The cook.

'Excuse me, good sir,' I said, 'we're delivering vegetables. The royal guard at the gate said you'd give us supper.'

'Did he?' the cook said with a scowl. 'Only the palace workers get fed from my kitchens.'

'But we're from the royal palace,' Drew put in. 'Tomorrow we will help set the tables and serve the king. Maybe you can let us sleep in the servants' hall tonight?'

The man blew out his apple-red cheeks. 'You'll come in useful. The bishop never has enough servants to help me. He's a mean old devil. Now get working. King's men or no king's men I'll beat you with a ladle if I see you skive.'

I thought of my Gladys and muttered, 'I'm used to that then.'

6

Pardon

The work was hard and the king was delayed by the mud on the roads. That made the cook bad tempered and he was lashing out with his ladle. It also meant it was dark by the time the bishop appeared in the hall to sit at the head of the table with King Athelstan. The bishop and all of his guests wore their finest robes and jewels that glittered in the light of fifty torches.

'When are you going to speak to the bishop?'

'When he's finished talking to the king,' I said.

'But that may be midnight. We need to get back to the village before the sun rises,' Drew hissed.

'I can't interrupt the king,' I groaned.

'Then I'll do it,' the old man said.

As the grey-haired bishop carved a huge salmon on the table in front of him, Drew stepped forward. 'Excuse me sir, but this is important.'

'How dare you, churl?' the bishop spat. 'You'll be arrested and thrown off the cliffs for your impertinence.'

As guards moved to grasp Drew by the arms he raised his voice, 'Your Grace, King Athelstan: hear me or a boy will die at first light.'

The king raised a hand and the guards loosed Drew. I was half hidden by a curtain. I wasn't afraid, of course. But there was no use us both dying, was there?

The king stroked his golden beard as the old watchman told the story of the dead sheep and the trial of Edward. 'We simply ask for your mercy on a poor boy.' At last

Drew fell silent. The hall was so silent we could hear the torches crackle on the walls.

At last King Athelstan spoke. 'I am not as sure of the boy's guilt as the magistrate seems to be. But even if the lad *did* kill his master's sheep he is too young to die. I will change the law of the land. No one under the age of sixteen years will hang, whatever his crime. Send for my clerk and I will write an order to the magistrate. The boy can be fined. He can work two weeks as a shepherd with no pay. That is punishment enough.' He looked at Drew. 'You did well, old man, to bring this case before me.'

'Thank you, your Grace, but it is dark and wild and we may not get back in time,' Drew sighed.

'Then the bishop will lend you a fine horse from his stables and I will send guards with torches to light your way and keep away robbers.'

'Two horses,' I said.

The king turned his sharp eyes on me. 'And you are?'

'Dear little Edwards's father, Your Grace,' I said.

King Athelstan gave a sharp nod. 'Be on your way. By the time your horses are saddled the letter will be sealed. Keep it safe.'

Even with the finest fastest horses in the south of England we struggled along the roads and through the moonless darkness. In the trees I was sure we'd be attacked by thieves or hobgoblins. Not that I was afraid. I was only worried they would delay us long enough for the rising sun to shine on my dear dead son.

The sky was lighter when we galloped into the village. Edward was being led from the village pound and the last nails were being hammered into the wooden scaffold tree. I reached inside my jerkin

with frozen fingers and waved the king's letter. 'A pardon,' I cried. 'The king himself has pardoned you.'

Some of the villagers gave out a sigh and moaned, 'No hanging for us today then.'

'Still at least we have a fair and a holiday,' another said.

Edward ran to my dear Gladys and she hugged him. She looked over the boy's head with the eyes of an adder and said, 'Get back to the house, Upton Medway. We need to talk.'

'I saved our son,' I wailed.

'You all but killed him,' she said. 'Home. Now.'

7
Truths

Gladys sat me by the door and handed me a shepherd's crook. 'You will go to Thane Hugh and tell him you are ready to start work.'

'I'm tired,' I whined. 'I've been riding all night.'

She ignored my plea. 'Lambing is about to start. There'll be lots of work. Lots of extra shepherds to guard the flocks at night.'

'I'm too old. I'll catch cold. I'll die.'

'And it'll serve you right.'

'Gladys, how can you say that? I saved

our son...'

'If you don't leave right now I will find the magistrate and tell him  who really killed the thane's sheep.'

'You know?' I said and my tired eyes must have been wide as one of the bishop's fine bowls.

'Yes. You left the house that night to take Edward some wood,' she said.

'Like a good father,' I sighed.

'You saw a stray sheep caught in the thorns of a hedge. You killed it. You hadn't the strength to bring it home so you cut off a leg and rolled the rest into the thorn bush.'

I hung my head. 'I wanted to feed my dear wife and son, like a good father.'

She waved her ladle at me. 'You let Edward take the blame. When he was sentenced to die you kept quiet. Like a bad father. The worst sort of father.'

'They'd have hanged me,' I moaned. 'I'm over sixteen. The king wouldn't have saved me.'

'You are also guilty. So nothing would save you. A nice tight noose might have stopped your complaining,' she said. 'You grumble and complain. You moan, you grouse, you gripe.'

'I hardly ever grumble,' I grumbled.

'And you never will again. If I hear one more moan from you I will go straight to the thane and tell him who really killed his sheep.'

'That is so unfair,' I sobbed.

'Was that a moan?' Gladys asked.

I gave a smile as faint as a new moon. 'No, my dearest. No.'

I threw back my shoulders and marched into the bitter wind. The best shepherd in the village was about to get back to work.

And I am not complaining. No. Honestly. I'm not.

Epilogue

This tale is based on a true story.

The people of Maidstone in Kent were cheated of an execution by King Athelstan. The king got to hear of the case of sheep-rustling Edward Medway. The starving boy had killed one of his own sheep and eaten its leg. He said the sheep was killed by wolves, but the leg had been neatly cut off and its throat slit. As the Maidstone magistrate said, 'I've never seen a wolf that carries a knife.'

The magistrate then sentenced

the sheep-killer to be hanged. Crowds had gathered from around the county and a fair had been set up in the square around the gallows.

Then came the sensational news. King Athelstan had changed the law so young criminals like Ed couldn't be killed.

The king wrote to Bishop Theodred and said,

It is not fair that a man should die so young. Or for such a small offence when he has seen others get away with it elsewhere.

The new law said that no one could be executed if they were under sixteen years of age.

So, young criminals couldn't be killed

in Saxon times. But by the Georgian age (the 1700s to the early 1800s) children were being executed again.

YOU TRY...

1. Plead for your life. Imagine you have been charged with stealing the head teacher's school dinner from the dining hall. Twenty people saw you do it. The head says you will be expelled from the school. You will lose all your best friends and go to a strange school. Can you write a letter to the head and plead with him or her. Tell them why you should NOT be expelled?

2. Life in a Saxon village was hard. Imagine you could travel back in time from your comfortable world of today. You can live a week in a Saxon village, like Edward's. What FIVE things would you take with you from today's world to help you survive?

3. Draw a large picture of a sheep.
Mark on SIX joints that people eat:

i) leg

ii) shoulder

iii) scrag

iv) loin

v) chump

vi) flank

Terry Deary's Saxon Tales

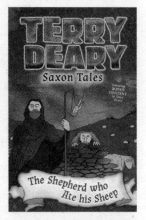

If you liked this book why not look out
for the rest of Terry Deary's Saxon Tales?